The Loneliest Whale

Written by Jessica Therrien

Illustrated by Dorene Uhrich

"For our boys." — Jessica & Dorene

www.acornpublishingLLC.com

ISBN 978-0-692-58134-6

This book belongs to:

_____

The Loneliest Whale
was a sad little lad.
He'd gone swimming alone
and lost his Dad.

So he sang their song
and hummed their tune,
hoping Dad would hear him soon.

Along came a turtle.

But the turtle couldn't speak whale,
so he hid inside a shoe.

"Can anybody hear me?" Little Whale called out.

A pig fish swam past him,
turning up his snout.

That octopus seems friendly, he thought as he swam on.

He whistled twice
to flag him down,
but the octopus was gone.

The scuttle of a crab made him turn, caught his eye.

"Hey," said The Lonely Whale, but the crab crawled on by.

His cry was a loud one,
ringing out through
the sea.

Please, I'm alone.

Can anyone hear me?

A shadow in the distance,
big, strong, and dark.
Little Whale got real quiet
as he watched a great white shark.

He whimpered and he whined.
"Why'd I leave my mom behind?"

All alone in the ocean
wasn't much fun.

"I wish I was with my dad,
swimming in the sun."

Then a sound so familiar
led him along sunken rocks.
His baby brother's laughter
from under the docks.

Little Whale waved a fin.
"Look, I found you.
I'm here."

Mom heard him and smiled.
"We missed you, my dear."

He swam toward his family
faster than fast.
The Loneliest Whale
had come home at last.

The
End

CPSIA information can be obtained
at www.ICGtesting.com
Printed in the USA
LVHW07n1834260318
571183LV00025B/1141/P